-My Family-
My Adopted Family

by Claudia Harrington
illustrated by Zoe Persico

Looking Glass Library

An Imprint of Magic Wagon
abdopublishing.com

Special thanks to Fran Young. —CH

To my passionate sisters that inspire me everyday from our shenanigans to their drive to achieve their dreams. —ZP

abdopublishing.com

Published by Magic Wagon, a division of ABDO, PO Box 398166, Minneapolis, Minnesota 55439. Copyright © 2018 by Abdo Consulting Group, Inc. International copyrights reserved in all countries. No part of this book may be reproduced in any form without written permission from the publisher. Looking Glass Library™ is a trademark and logo of Magic Wagon.

Printed in the United States of America, North Mankato, Minnesota.
052017
092017

THIS BOOK CONTAINS
RECYCLED MATERIALS

Written by Claudia Harrington
Illustrated by Zoe Persico
Edited by Heidi M.D. Elston
Art Directed by Candice Keimig

Publisher's Cataloging-in-Publication Data

Names: Harrington, Claudia, author. | Persico, Zoe, illustrator.
Title: My adopted family / by Claudia Harrington ; illustrated by Zoe Persico.
Description: Minneapolis, MN : Magic Wagon, 2018. | Series: My family
Summary: Lenny follows Adam for a school project and learns what it's like to be
     part of an adopted family.
Identifiers: LCCN 2017930511 | ISBN 9781532130168 (lib. bdg.) |
     ISBN 9781614798316 (ebook) | ISBN 9781614798385 (Read-to-me ebook)
Subjects: LCSH: Family--Juvenile fiction. | Family life--Juvenile fiction. |
     Adoption--Juvenile fiction.
Classification: DDC [E]--dc23
LC record available at http://lccn.loc.gov/2017930511

"Get your backpacks ready," said Miss Fish at the end of the day. "Lenny, when the bell rings, you may leave with Adam. He's Student of the Week."
"Thanks," said Lenny, getting the camera.

When the bell rang, Adam didn't move.

"Are we going?" asked Lenny.

"We have to wait for my little sister, Emily," said Adam.

A first grader cartwheeled into Adam's hug.

Click!

"Will you carry my stuff?" Emily asked. "It's too heavy. Who's this?" she said, turning to stare at Lenny.

Adam's knees buckled under the weight of the bags. "This is my friend Lenny. He's coming to our house."

"Hi, Lenny," said Emily.

"Hey," said Lenny. "How do you get home?"
Lenny asked Adam.

Emily vaulted onto Lenny's back. "Piggyback!"

"Oof," said Lenny. He pretended he was a horse.

Adam walked behind them, lugging all the bags.

"This is a GOOD friend," said Emily. "Giddyup!"

"This is a tired friend," Lenny said when they'd gone four blocks.

Emily slid off.

"Good timing," said Adam. "This is it!"
Click!

"Do you get something to drink when you get home?" panted Lenny as they staggered inside.

"Smoothies coming up," whispered a man on the phone. "I'll be right off."

"Dad works from home," Adam explained.

Click!

"Does he make you do homework right away?" asked Lenny as they got their smoothies. **Click!**

"Nah," said Adam. "Mom does that. She'll be home soon. She teaches high school. Want to go outside and do some gymnastics?"

Emily grabbed Lenny's camera. "Smile!"

Click!

Lenny's arms shook. "Who gets you down?" he asked after two wobbly swings.

"Watch, Lenny!" screamed Emily as she walked the balance beam.
"Whoooooa," said Lenny, starting to slip.

"Just jump," said Adam. "You can almost touch."

"Hi, kids!" Adam's mom greeted them as she walked outside.

Click!

"You must be Lenny. I see Adam is trying to turn you into a gymnast." She winked at Lenny.

"Guess what, Mom?" said Adam.
"I nailed my first kip on the bar!"
"Great," said Mom. "Time to
celebrate. With homework!"
"Awww, Mom," said Adam.

Mom laughed. "What do you have tonight?"

"All About Me!" the boys said.

"Like favorite food. PIZZA! Hint, hint," said Adam.

"Sorry," said Mom. "It's stir-fry tonight.

Lenny, your mom said it was okay if you

joined us for dinner."

"Cool," said Lenny. "Who makes it?"

"Dad starts, so Mom can grade papers," said Adam. "Then she fixes it."

"Hardy har har," said Dad. He tossed them each a snow pea.

Click!

"Hey, Mom!" said Adam. "Can I use this photo of when I first chose you? We're supposed to glue on a baby picture."

"Sure." She kissed his head.

"Remember, we chose you, too."

"Huh?" asked Lenny.

"Emily and I were adopted," said Adam.

"Cool," said Lenny.

When they finished homework and dinner,
Adam showed Lenny his room.
"Wow!" said Lenny. "Bunk beds!
Do you get the top?"
Click!

"Yeah, it's cool, except when Emily snores,"
teased Adam.

"Do not!" said Emily.

"Who tucks you in?" asked Lenny as his mom came in with Adam's parents.
"Mom reads to us first," said Adam. "Then Dad tells us about when he went to the Olympics."

"In a cast!" said Adam's dad, winking.

"I won't go skiing before *my* Olympics," said Adam.

They all laughed.

Lenny yawned. "Who loves you best?"

"I do," said Adam's mom. "Around the high bar five times!"

"Me, too," said his dad. "With a triple flip dismount!"

"Me, three!" said Emily, climbing sleepily into Adam's hug.
Click!

"Me, four!" said Lenny's mom, hugging him.

Adam high-fived Lenny as Emily waved.

"See you tomorrow, future star Olympian," said Lenny.

"Tomorrow, future ace reporter," Adam replied.